OTIS
THE ROBOT

supply teacher

Jim Carrington • **Juanbjuan Oliver**

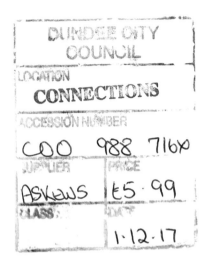
Otis the Robot meets a supply teacher

ISBN: 978-1-85503-608-6

© Jim Carrington 2017
Illustrations by Juanbjuan Oliver / Beehive Illustration

This edition published 2017
10 9 8 7 6 5 4 3 2 1

Printed in the UK by Page Bros (Norwich) Ltd
Designed and typeset by Andy Wilson for Green Desert Ltd

LDA, Findel Education, 2 Gregory Street, Hyde, Cheshire SK14 4HR

www.ldalearning.com

Hi! My name is Otis. I am a robot.

I go to Roboschool every day
except weekends, holidays
and when I'm ill.

I like school. But I **don't** like it when things change... like today at school.

Mrs A-Bot wasn't there.
Instead, there was a
different teacher.
'Hello, Otis,' he said.
'I'm Mr Sirkits.'

I didn't speak to him. I didn't know
who he was or how he knew my name.
My circuits felt **prickly**.

I was worried.

'Could you come
and sit on the
carpet with us?'
he said.

6

But I didn't want to
sit on the carpet.
I didn't want to do
anything. I wanted
Mrs A-Bot back,
and for everything
to be normal.

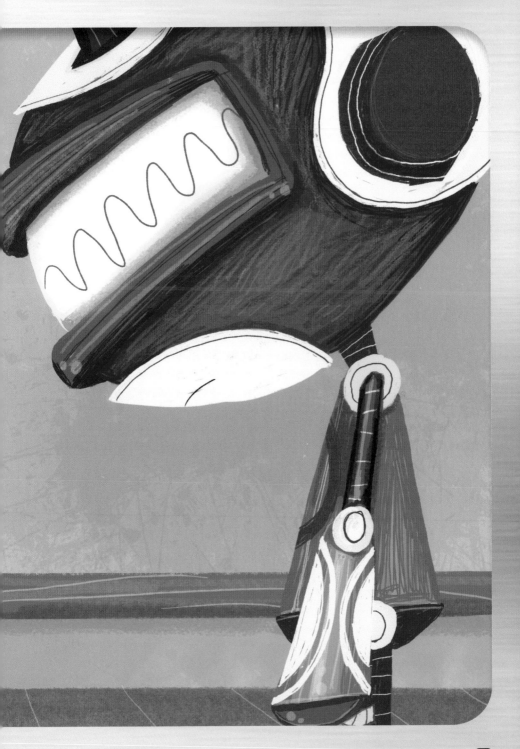

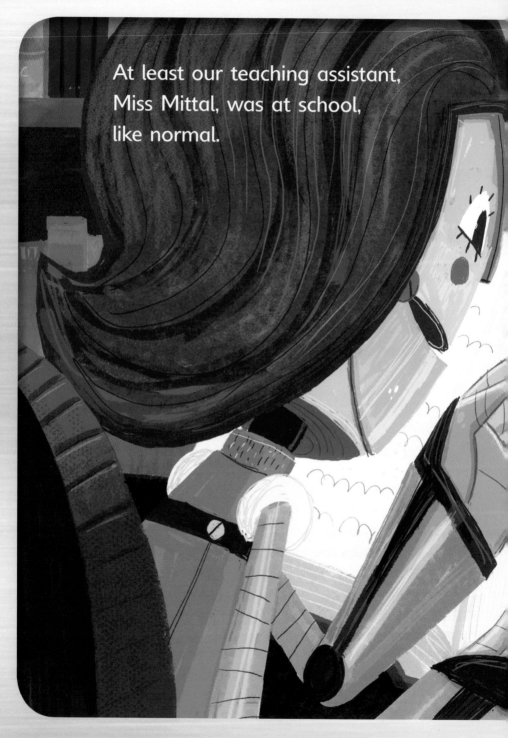

At least our teaching assistant,
Miss Mittal, was at school,
like normal.

'Let's have a look at what **The Manual** says,' she said.

11

When we'd finished reading **The Manual**, Miss Mittal said, 'Mrs A-Bot was too ill to come to school today.'

'But I know that Mr Sirkits is a really good teacher . . . and he loves computers, just like you!'

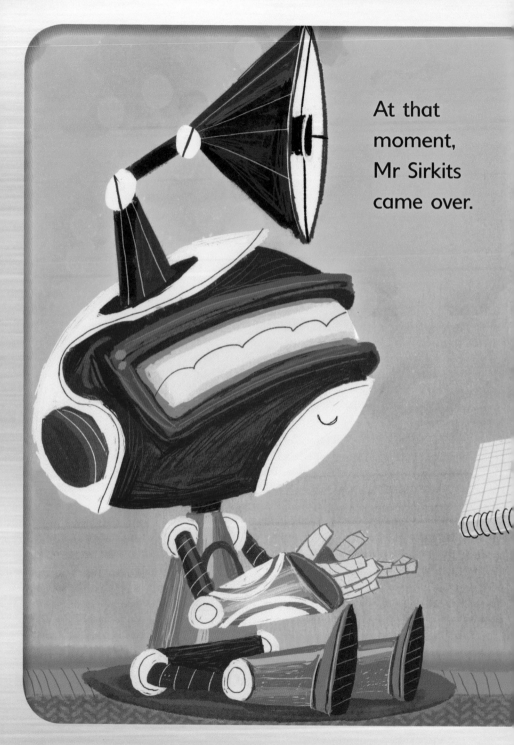

At that
moment,
Mr Sirkits
came over.

'Otis, would you like to come and do some work with me?

When you're finished you can have a reward.'

Mr Sirkits helped me write the **best** story I've ever written.

It was about an astronaut called Otis who took his **ROCKET SHIP** to explore all the planets in the solar system.

I drew a picture to go with it.

17

Mr Sirkits
gave me
a sticker.
'*Super*
work, Otis,'
he said.

'What would you
like to do as
a reward?'

19

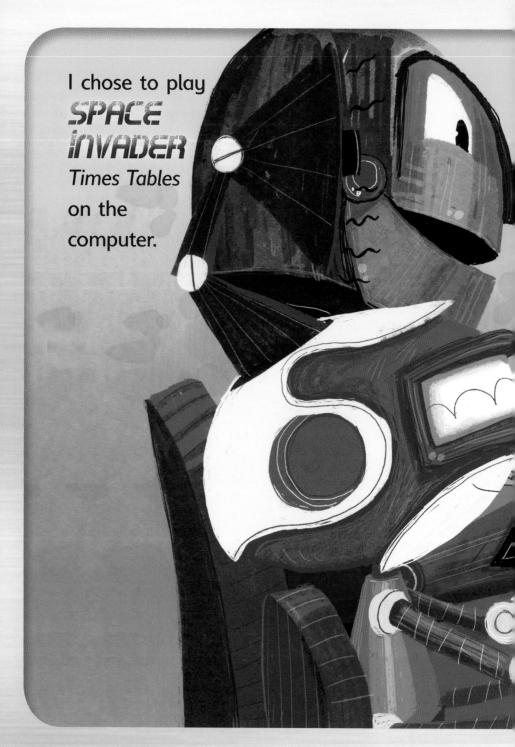

I chose to play
SPACE INVADER
Times Tables
on the
computer.

'Brilliant choice,' Mr Sirkits said. 'Can I play too?' My circuits felt **warm** and happy.

What to do if I have a supply teacher
(from Otis the Robot meets a supply teacher)

I go to school most days. My teacher is called Mrs A-Bot.

My teacher takes my class every day that we are at school.

But sometimes my teacher is ill or on a course and can't come to school.

Then we have another teacher. Sometimes this is a teacher I know and sometimes it is a supply teacher. All the teachers know what to teach us. Just like Mrs A-Bot.

Having a teacher who is not my usual teacher makes me feel nervous.

Sometimes, when I feel nervous, I don't do my work.

The school only chooses teachers who will be kind and help us to learn. I don't need to be nervous about a new teacher.

It is good to meet new people. It can be fun for me and for them too. The new teacher will be told how to help all the children, including me. This is good.

There are also other adults in my school who I know and who I can ask for help if I am worried.

My teacher will come back to school when they are feeling well again.